nickelodeon

ꙮ AMAZING ADVENTURES! ꙮ

A Random House PICTUREBACK® Book

Random House 🏠 New York

© 2018 Viacom International Inc. All rights reserved. Published in the United States by Random House Children's Books, a division of Penguin Random House LLC, 1745 Broadway, New York, NY 10019, and in Canada by Penguin Random House Canada Limited, Toronto. Originally published in slightly different form by Random House Books for Young Readers as *Sparkle Fest Showdown!* in 2017, adapted by Mickie Matheis, and *The Great Egg Race!* in 2018, adapted by Courtney Carbone. Pictureback, Random House, and the Random House colophon are registered trademarks of Penguin Random House LLC. Nickelodeon, Nick Jr., Nella the Princess Knight, and all related titles, logos, and characters are trademarks of Viacom International Inc.
rhcbooks.com
ISBN 978-0-375-97763-3
Printed in the United States of America
10 9 8 7 6 5 4 3 2 1

One sunny day, Princess Nella and her best friend, Sir Garrett, were in Castlehaven's town square, admiring the shiny balloons and glittery banners that decorated the kingdom. The townspeople were celebrating Sparkle Fest.

"It's absolutely, positively my favorite holiday *ever*!" exclaimed Nella.

Every year, one horse from the kingdom was named Sparkle Fest Champion. The winner had the honor of pulling Nella's family to the castle in the royal carriage for the Sparkle Fest Light Show. "I wonder who the next Sparkle Fest Champion will be!" the princess said excitedly.

"I sure hope it's *meeeee!*" said Nella's best unicorn friend, Trinket. "Being *sparkle*-tastic is my *thing!*"

"Being Sparkle Fest Champion isn't just about being sparkly—it's also about having fun," Nella reminded Trinket.

"Totally, Nella," said Trinket. "Of course."

The competition was about to start when everyone heard a loud crash. Sir Garrett's horse, Clod, rushing over to enter the contest, had tripped and fallen into a flower bed.

Nella and Garrett giggled at the silly horse.

"Glad you could make it, Clod," the princess said with a smile.

Trinket was surprised to learn that Clod was trying out to be Sparkle Fest Champion. He wasn't sparkly at all!

"Being Sparkle Fest Champion is *my* thing," said Trinket. "*I'm* the sparkly one."

The first event was the Prance-Off, where the horses danced their way across the stage. Tossing her shiny mane, Trinket dazzled the crowd with her perfect rhythm.

Clod came next, and his dancing left the crowd speechless. His hooves moved wildly in every direction. But he looked like he was having a great time.

Trinket was pronounced the winner of the Prance-Off, and Clod congratulated her enthusiastically. "Good job, Trinket!" he said. "That was so fun! The Speed Race is next. Race you to the track!"

When Clod sped away, he immediately stepped into a flowerpot. He didn't even notice that it was stuck to his hoof. Nella and Garrett giggled as the horses lined up to race.

Nella raised her hand. "On your marks, get set, GO!"

Clod was so busy talking about how much he loved running, he didn't realize the other horses had sprinted away.

During the race, Clod was far behind the others. Then he noticed an ice cream cart at the end of the track. He made a mad dash for it—leaving the other horses in a cloud of dust!

"Clod is our winner!" Nella announced to the cheering crowd.

Trinket was stunned. Whoever won the third and final event would be named Sparkle Fest Champion.

Clod trotted over to her. "Hey, Trinket, I just wanted to say I'm having so much fun with you today."

But Trinket wasn't having fun. How could she have fun if she didn't win?

The last event was a jumping contest. Trinket and Clod put on an awesome show! Clod wowed the crowd with his rock-star moves while Trinket enchanted them with her fancy dance poses.

She did her best. But would it be enough? She'd have to wait and see what the judges decided.

Nella held up her hands to quiet the crowd. "This year's Sparkle Fest Champion is . . . TRINKET!" she said.

Trinket twirled around with delight.

". . . AND CLOD!" Nella continued. "It's a tie!"

Clod was thrilled, but Trinket couldn't believe her ears. Being Sparkle Fest Champion was her *thing*! She didn't want to share it with Clod.

When it was almost time for the light show, Nella
hitched Trinket and Clod to the royal carriage. A pretty
ribbon connected their harnesses.

"Okay, your harnesses are attached, and you're ready
to go. Have fun!" Nella told them. King Dad, Queen
Mom, and Princess Norma climbed into the carriage.

Clod was so happy to be next to Trinket.

"Look at us!" he said. "One little ribbon holding together two Sparkle Fest buddies! Gosh, without that ribbon, you'd be pulling this carriage all alone."

"Really?" Trinket said. That gave her an idea. "Clod, look over there—a kitten!"

When Clod looked away, Trinket pulled the flimsy ribbon loose and quickly trotted off with the carriage.

Watching from the grandstand, Nella called, "Trinket! You're leaving Clod behind!"

Trinket looked back to see Clod's sad face. Even though she really wanted to be the only Sparkle Fest Champion, she couldn't leave her friend.

But when she tried to stop the carriage, the harness snapped!

"Oh, no! Help!" Trinket cried as the carriage rolled away with the royal family inside.

"I'm coming!" Clod said.

"Hold on, Trinket!" Nella called as her Knightly Heart necklace began to glow. The townspeople watched in amazement as Nella transformed into a Princess Knight, sparkly and strong.

Nella had to act fast to save her parents and baby sister! She tossed her sword into the air, and it turned into a bow with a brightly colored ribbon.

She grabbed an arrow and shot it into a tree branch, then used the ribbon to swing down from the grandstand.

Nella landed on her feet on the backs of Trinket and Clod. She gripped their reins and charged after the runaway carriage.

"Thank goodness you're here!" Trinket said, relieved. "I'm so sorry! I made a big mistake!"

"It's okay, Trinket," Nella said. "Right now we have to work together to fix this. Follow that carriage!"

Just as they were gaining on the carriage, it hit a rock, which made it turn sharply and barrel down a steep hillside! Nella, Trinket, and Clod charged after the carriage.

"Hold on, Mom and Dad!" Nella called. "We're coming!"

Trinket and Clod finally caught up to the carriage. Nella quickly reattached their harnesses to it just in time. They were heading straight toward a ravine!

Nella thought quickly. "We have to jump over the ravine!"

"We'll never make it!" Trinket protested.

"Yes, we will," Nella replied. "It's like the Jumping Contest—you guys were great at that. But you have to work together as a team. Get ready—on the count of three. One . . . two . . . THREE!"

With that, Trinket and Clod leapt over the ravine. The horses and the carriage landed safely on the other side.

"Way to go!" Nella cheered.
"We did it!" Clod said.
"And doing it together was actually . . . *fun*!" Trinket added.

With the royal family safe, Nella and her
friends hurried to the castle for the light show.
"Would you like to do the honors?" Nella
asked Trinket and Clod.
Smiling happily, the pair flipped the switch
together, lighting up the castle in a brilliant
display of color.
It was the best, brightest Sparkle Fest ever!

THE GREAT EGG RACE!

One sunny morning, Nella, Sir Garrett, and Sir Blaine were playing Follow the Knight. Sir Blaine was showing off.

"When it comes to doing knightly things," he said, "this knight always wins!"

Suddenly, a dragon passed overhead!

Nella's parents, Queen Mom and King Dad, ran out of the castle.

"I've never seen a dragon like *that* before!" Nella exclaimed.

"That's because it's a Pink Polka-Dotted Mountain Dragon!" said King Dad.

Sir Garrett read his Knightly Trading Card about the dragon.

"No one has ever seen a Pink Polka-Dotted Mountain Dragon egg hatch before," he said.

Queen Mom told them that the first person who did would get a special Dragon Medal!

"Then I shall be that knight!" Sir Blaine said. He ran off to find a Pink Polka-Dotted Mountain Dragon egg.

Nella and Sir Garrett wanted to see the egg hatch, too. Nella's tiara began to glow as she magically transformed into a Princess Knight. Now she was ready for anything!

Nella led the way to Pink Polka-Dotted Mountain to find the dragon's nest.

When they reached the mountain, Nella and
Sir Garrett found Sir Blaine standing at the edge
of an enormous pit.

Sir Blaine grabbed a hanging vine and swung
across the pit. He landed safely on the other side.

"Ha!" he called to the others, laughing.
"I'm the best!"

"It's going to be impossible to catch up with Sir Blaine now," Sir Garrett said.

"Not for a Princess Knight!" exclaimed Nella. She transformed her sword into a bow and fired two ribbon arrows into a tree. Then she and Sir Garrett grabbed hold of the ribbons and swung themselves across the pit.

Nella and Sir Garrett reached the top of the mountain. They found a dragon's nest holding a large pink polka-dotted egg. But Sir Blaine was already there.

"I got here first!" he shouted. "Let's hear it for Sir Blaine!" As he danced around in celebration, he accidentally knocked the egg out of the nest!

"Stop that egg!" Nella cried.
    They all hopped onto her shield, using it like a
snowboard to quickly slide down the mountain. But
the egg slid even faster . . . right off the edge of a cliff!

Splash!
The egg landed in a river.
"We've got to stop that egg before it hits those rocks!" Nella said.
But Sir Blaine wanted to save the egg by himself so he could see it hatch and win the medal. He ran ahead.

Nella realized that the only way to get Sir Blaine to help was to turn the rescue into a contest.

"Last one to the rocks is a swamp slug!" she shouted.

"You're on!" Sir Blaine called back, racing her and Sir Garrett to the riverbank.

When they'd all reached the rocks, Nella said to Sir Blaine, "I bet you can't jump to the other side!" He did, and then she tossed him one end of a ribbon. She challenged him to a game of tug-of-war. As they pulled back and forth, the ribbon stopped the egg from hitting the rocks!

"We saved the egg!" Sir Blaine crowed. Then he realized what he'd said.

"Yup," said Sir Garrett. "You guys worked together."

"And together we need to get this egg back to its nest," Nella declared.

Just then, the mother dragon arrived.
Sir Blaine was scared, but Nella stepped forward.
"Sorry about that, Mrs. Dragon. We didn't mean to
knock your egg out of the nest. We did our best to
keep it safe."
The mother dragon was so relieved to see that
her egg was okay that she offered to fly Nella,
Sir Garrett, and Sir Blaine back to the castle!

After they had landed, Nella introduced Mrs. Dragon to King Dad and Queen Mom. Then the dragon egg began to crack! An adorable Pink Polka-Dotted Mountain Dragon baby popped out of the shell.

"I saw it first—I win!" said Sir Blaine, grabbing the medal. Everyone stared at him, shocked. "Well . . . I guess we all sort of saw it at the same time."

"Which means we *all* won!" cheered Nella, taking the other side of the medal to raise it into the air.

Even Sir Blaine had to agree. They had all won because they had worked together.

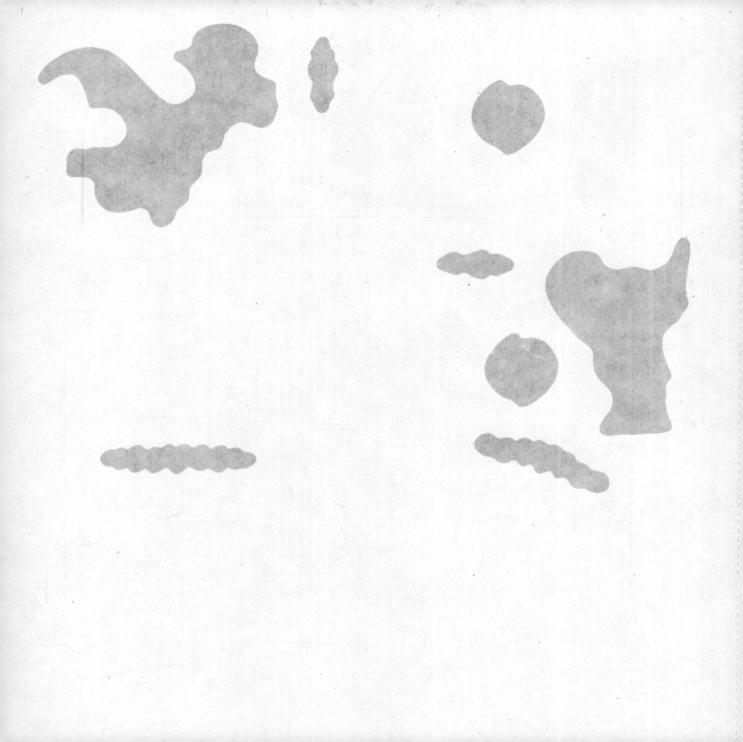